My First
Disney Princess
LIBRARY

The Magic of Dreams

PaRRagon

Bath · New York · Singapore · Hong Kong · Cologne · Delhi
Melbourne · Amsterdam · Johannesburg · Auckland · Shenzhen

This edition published by Parragon in 2010

Parragon
Queen Street House
4 Queen Street
Bath BA1 1HE, UK

Adapted by Andrea Nikki Grimes
Illustrated Disney Storybook Artists
Designed by Kar Heng Goh

ISBN 978-1-4454-2408-8
Printed in China

The Magic of Dreams

Nikki Grimes

Once upon a time, a wealthy widower lived in a fine house with his daughter, Cinderella. He loved his daughter very much and gave her many beautiful things. Still, he felt Cinderella should have a mother's care, so he married a woman with two young daughters who were just about Cinderella's age.

Sadly, Cinderella's father died soon after he married. It was not long until Cinderella discovered that her Stepmother was a cold and cruel woman.

As the years passed, Cinderella's Stepmother spoiled her two daughters. Anastasia and Drizella slept in large, lovely bedrooms, while Cinderella was given a tiny room in the attic. And while her stepsisters lived like princesses, poor Cinderella was forced to do the washing, serve meals, and clean the house—just like a servant!

Despite her family's cruelty, Cinderella remained kind and gentle. All of the animals loved her. She took special care of her dog, Bruno, and brushed her old horse each day. The birds sang for her, and the mice were always there to keep her company. In fact, Cinderella made tiny clothes for the mice, and often rescued them from the claws of her Stepmother's nasty cat, Lucifer.

Early one morning, Cinderella sat at the window in her tiny room and stared out at the castle in the distance. She dreamed of one day wearing a beautiful gown and dancing at a fancy ball. 'Some day, my dreams will come true,' she said to herself.

Suddenly, Cinderella's Stepmother called for her.

'Coming, Stepmother!' Cinderella answered.

Meanwhile, the King had troubles of his own. He wanted his son to marry right away, but the Prince wanted to wait for the girl of his dreams.

The King had an idea. He told the Grand Duke that they would have a ball and invite all of the young women in the kingdom. The Prince would surely find a wife there!

The invitations were delivered that very day. When the messenger delivered an invitation to Cinderella's house, she answered the door. 'This arrived from the palace,' Cinderella said as she handed the invitation to her Stepmother.

As the Stepmother read the invitation aloud, Anastasia and Drizella jumped with excitement. Cinderella asked if she could go, too.

'You may go,' her Stepmother said sternly, 'if you finish all your chores and find something suitable to wear.'

Cinderella ran to her room and found an old ball gown. Maybe it's a little old-fashioned, she thought to herself, but I'll fix that. She then pulled out her book of dress patterns, to look for a lovely new design.

Then Cinderella remembered she had chores to do. She started on them straight away, working as quickly as she could. But as soon as she finished one task, she was given another.

It was eight o'clock at night when Cinderella finally completed the last chore. She dragged herself up to her dark room, tired and sad. There was no time left to finish her ball gown.

As Cinderella entered the room, however, her animal friends opened her closet door. Inside hung her ball gown, finished to look just like the one in the pattern book. The birds and mice had done all the sewing!

'Oh, thank you so much!' Cinderella said with joy. She quickly got dressed and rushed downstairs to join her stepsisters.

But when Cinderella found her stepsisters, they were not happy.
Anastasia and Drizella saw that Cinderella was wearing a sash and beads
that had once belonged to them. They ripped the gown to shreds while
their mother watched.

'Girls, girls,' the Stepmother said once the gown was ripped beyond
repair. 'That's enough. Hurry along now. Goodnight, Cinderella.'

Sobbing, Cinderella ran into the garden. 'It's no use,' she cried. She thought that her dreams would never come true.

Suddenly, the garden filled with light. Cinderella looked up to see her Fairy Godmother.

'Come now, dry those tears,' the kind fairy said. 'You can't go to the ball looking like that.'

With a wave of her wand, the Fairy Godmother turned a pumpkin into a glittering coach and she turned the mice into horses. She then waved her wand again, and changed the horse into a coachman and Bruno the dog into a footman.

Last of all, the Fairy Godmother transformed Cinderella's rags into a lovely ball gown and put glass slippers on her tiny feet.

Cinderella twirled around in her beautiful new gown. 'It's like a dream!' she said with a sigh.

'Yes, my child,' answered the Fairy Godmother. 'But you'll only have until midnight. On the stroke of twelve, the spell will be broken and everything will be as it was before.'

And with that, Cinderella stepped into the coach and was whisked away to the ball.

When Cinderella entered the ballroom, the Prince rushed over and asked her to dance. Cinderella smiled and took his hand. They danced all night, and everyone could see that they were falling in love.

'Who is she, Mother?' asked Drizella. None of Cinderella's family had recognised her.

Suddenly, the clock struck twelve. 'Oh dear!' said Cinderella. 'It's midnight! I must leave.' And she broke away from the Prince.

'Wait!' called the Prince. 'I don't even know your name! How will I find you?'

But Cinderella could only hear the clock chiming. She ran away.

As Cinderella fled, the Grand Duke ran after her. He knew that the Prince had finally found the maiden he wanted to marry, and the King would be furious if she got away.

Racing down the stairs, Cinderella lost a glass slipper. A few steps behind, the Grand Duke stopped to pick it up. But when he looked around a moment later, Cinderella was gone.

Just beyond the palace gates, at the last stroke of midnight, the spell was broken. Just as the Fairy Godmother had said, everything returned to how it had been before. Everything, that is, except for the tiny glass slipper on Cinderella's foot. She took the slipper off and carried it home.

The next day, the King frantically listened as the Grand Duke told him, 'The Prince is determined to marry none but the girl who fits the slipper.' And so the King sent the Grand Duke out into the town, to try the slipper on every young maiden and find out who the girl from the ball was.

When Cinderella's Stepmother heard of the Grand Duke's search, she was determined that Anastasia or Drizella be chosen to marry the Prince. She knew that Cinderella was fairer than her daughters, so she decided that she must not have a chance to try on the slipper. The Stepmother quickly locked Cinderella in her room.

But Cinderella wasn't locked in for long. The mice stole the key, carried it upstairs, and slipped it under Cinderella's door.

When the Grand Duke arrived at the house, Anastasia and Drizella tried to force their big feet into the tiny glass slipper. But it was no use. Then, just as the Grand Duke was about to leave, Cinderella appeared at the top of the stairs. 'May I try it on?' she asked.

As the footman carried the slipper towards Cinderella, her Stepmother tripped him! The glass slipper crashed down onto the floor, shattering into a thousand pieces.

Just as the Grand Duke was about to panic, Cinderella interrupted. 'I have the other slipper,' she said with a smile. And she pulled the remaining glass slipper from under her apron.

The Grand Duke knelt before Cinderella and eased the slipper onto her dainty foot. It was a perfect fit!

Soon, Cinderella and the Prince were married. And they lived happily ever after.

The End